The Dreaded Noodle-Doodles

You, me
and
Thing

You, Me and Thing:

The Dreaded Noodle-Doodles

You, me and Thing

Karen McCombie

Illustrated by Alex T. Smith

faber and faber

First published in 2012
by Faber and Faber Limited
Bloomsbury House,
74–77 Great Russell Street,
London, WC1B 3DA

Typeset by Faber and Faber
Printed in England by CPI Group (UK) Ltd, Croydon, CR0 4YY

A CIP record for this book
is available from the British Library

ISBN 978–0–571–27259–4

FSC
www.fsc.org
MIX
Paper from
responsible sources
FSC® C101712

2 4 6 8 10 9 7 5 3 1

For Lettice,
because she's lovely!

Contents

A very secret Thing

Want to know a secret?

There is something very, *very* strange living in the trees behind my house.

If you tiptoe *slowwwwly* and quietly (shh!) to the bottom of my garden, you might hear it rustling and rootling and 'peh!'ing in the dark undergrowth, on the other side of the low stone wall.

And if you peek over the wall – holding

your breath – there's a chance you could
spot two saucer-round eyes blinking out of a
strangely square opening in the tree roots . . .

Oops – hope I haven't scared you.

'Cause *I'm* not.

Scared, I mean.

And here's why: the something at the
bottom of my garden is a friendly little thing
called, er, *Thing*.

So what *is* Thing?

Good question.

I'm not sure. Neither is my friend (and neighbour) Jackson.

It's as if someone put a troll, a fairy and a squirrel in a blender and Thing was what tumbled out once all the whirring stopped.

'So, Ruby, why don't you and Jackson take, er, *Thing* to a vet, to find out what it *is* exactly?' you might well ask.

Ah, but there's a problem . . .

If we took Thing to a vet, the vet might panic and *immediately* phone the newspapers or important government scientists or someone.

And then Thing wouldn't be our special secret any more; it would get snatched away from me and Jackson and its hideaway home in the tree roots, which would be completely terrible and frightening and *awful* for Thing. (*And* us.)

Or the vet might just faint with shock when it started talking.

Oh, yes. Thing can talk.

It can chatter away in human, rabbit, starling and slug, and the language of every *other* type of creature that happened to stroll, hop, flap or ooze around the deep, dark forest where it used to live.

(By the way, the deep, dark forest was called Muir Woods. It's now a big, blocky housing estate called Forest View Homes.)

Speaking tricky languages is an amazing talent to have, I know, but Thing isn't exactly *fluent* in them. Not in human, at least.

I mean, when I asked it about the weird stubby wings on its back a few days ago, it answered, in its funny, purry voice, 'Wingles not *ever* work, Rubby.'

See what I mean?

And its being able to talk hasn't helped me and Jackson learn very much about Thing. We've tried asking it questions like

'Are you a boy or a
girl thing?' and 'How old
are you?', and all it answers is
'Not *know*, thank you'.

Now you might think Thing
sounds quite cute, and it is. (Even
if it can't ever pronounce my name
properly.)

But we do have one *tiny* little
problem with it.

In fact, we *nearly* had a
tiny little problem the
other day, when I was
asking Thing about its

wingles. It *nearly* happened because Jackson was making these dopey flapping actions with his hands behind Thing's back.

Luckily, Thing didn't spot him, or it might have thought Jackson was taking the mickey (he was).

And if it thought Jackson was taking the mickey, it would've got upset.

And when Thing gets upset, it feels a bit ARRGHH!

And when Thing feels a bit ARRGHH!, *that's* when you've got to worry.

Just like last week when . . .

Oh, it's a long story.

Let's just say Thing got us into some very noodly, doodly and totally *dreadful* trouble . . .

2

A dangerous swish . . .

This story might *end* with noodles, doodles and total dreadfulness, but it *begins* with a swish.

Yes, a swish.

(Don't worry; I'll explain as we go along.)

Let's go back, back, back in time. All the way to last Monday, straight after school.

As usual, me and Jackson had told our parents that we were going to hang out together. But then quicketty-quick, we scuttled off to the straggle of trees – all that's left of Muir Woods – at the bottom of both our gardens.

'Hello, Thing!' I called out softly, as I jumped over the low stone wall, only *slightly* squashing the mushrooms I'd smuggled out of the fridge and hidden in my pocket.

'Hi, Thing!' said Jackson, vaulting over the higher fence of *his* garden.

Thing lifted a paw and flapped a hello at us.

It was hunkered down in the entrance to its rabbit-hole-sized cave, rocking from side to side and singing some odd little song that sounded a lot like 'Swish – swish! Swishy – swishy – swish!'

Me and Jackson, we didn't so much hunker as jiggle, trying to find ourselves a piece of ground that didn't have any bottom-bothering tree-root knobbles.

'Check this out: Miss Wilson marked me

really badly,' Jackson sighed, as he finally found a comfy-ish spot, and flung open a work-book.

He looked as crumpled as the scrunched-up rucksack by his side.

He also seemed truly shocked that our teacher had given his geography homework just two out of ten.

I wasn't. In fact, I thought he'd been pretty *lucky* to get two out of ten!

'Jackson, I spent an hour and a half on *my* homework, and it was 200 words long by the time I'd finished,' I told him, while passing dented mushrooms to Thing. 'You told me it took you *five minutes* to do, and the heating instructions on a tin of soup are longer than what *you've* written!'

'**Swish –swish –swish –swish –swish!**' Thing carried on sing-songing to itself, between nibbles of its favourite food (not

9

counting jelly babies, of course).

'But Ruby, I'm just no *good* at writing!' Jackson whined uselessly.

'Jackson, what you're not very good at is *trying*,' I told him sternly, realising that I suddenly sounded exactly like Miss Wilson.

It was only a few weeks ago that Jackson

had started at our school, and our teacher
had spent a lot of time saying the same
few words over and over again to him, like
'concentrate', 'pay' and 'attention'.

'I *do* try, Ruby!' Jackson whined some
more, looking hurt. 'And I am good at *some*
stuff!'

Oh, yeah. Jackson is good at . . .

- being cheeky
- teasing me
- making rude noises with his hand and his armpit, and
- generally acting like a big baboon.

'And I bet tomorrow's test is going to be *way* too hard!' he carried on moaning, rustling his hand in the packet of jelly babies by his side.

(Oh, yeah . . . that's something *else* Jackson is good at – throwing jelly babies in the air and catching them in his mouth. Slurp.)

'Well, that's all right – you've got tonight to study for the test!' I reminded him.

Jackson pulled a face at me, as if I'd just suggested something crazy like painting his face bright blue.

'Rubby?' interrupted Thing. It had stopped singing its swishy song and was pointing a mushroom at Jackson.

'Yes?' I said to our small, ginger-furred buddy.

'What is wrong with boy's *head*, please?'

We both stared at Thing and Thing stared at Jackson.

I wasn't sure what the problem was, exactly. Glancing at Jackson, all I saw was floppy blond hair, a dumb expression, and a

smattering of freckles across his nose. Wait a
minute; was *that* what Thing meant?

'Oh, those are freckles,' I began to explain,
helping myself to a jellybaby from Jackson's
open packet. 'They're just darker skin
markings. They don't—'

'Peh. No, *not* spotties,' sighed Thing,
stepping down from the strangely square
entrance to his cave and pitter-pattering
across to Jackson.

(By the way, Thing's home isn't *actually*
a cave. It's an old Scooby-Doo Mystery
Machine toy van that once belonged to
Jackson. Of course we've camouflaged it with
moss and twigs and woodlice and stuff.)

'See? Big line on head *here*,' Thing purred,
tapping a half-nibbled mushroom on
Jackson's forehead.

'Oh, *that*! That's a frown,' I told it.

'But what it's *for*, Rubby?' asked Thing,

as Jackson relaxed and the frown did a vanishing act.

Thing jumped in surprise, as if it had just seen an amazing conjuring trick.

'Well, frowns happen when humans are worried,' I carried on, 'and Jackson is a bit worried about a geography test we're having at school tomorrow.'

'*School . . .*' muttered Thing thoughtfully, as it dropped the mushroom and made a grab for the tight skin on Jackson's forehead, squishing it together with its fingers to make a DIY frown.

(Jackson 'oww!'ed and winced.)

'Yes, *school*,' I repeated, leaning over and unclipping Thing's grip,

then offering it the bag of
jelly babies to distract it.
'That's where children go to
learn lots of stuff, remember.
Is there something else you
want to know about school?'

'Yes, *please*, Rubby.' Thing nodded,
choosing a red jellybaby and delicately
biting its head off. 'Is it like big, big *wood*?'

Ah.

Until they got chopped down, Thing had
spent the whole of its life surrounded by
hundreds and hundreds of trees. Which made
trying to describe *anything* in the outside
world very tricky. A couple of days before, I'd
had a go at describing a library, but in the
end I *still* think Thing imagined it as some
kind of forest with books balancing along
branches, like some fluttery, rectangular fruit.

'No, school is *not* a wood,' I replied. 'It's

like a house, only much, *much* bigger.'

'A buildinging?' Thing checked. It was probably frowning without realising under its fur. Thing didn't like modern building(ing)s – after all, they were the reason its home and Muir Woods didn't exist any more.

'Yes, but an *old* building, like mine,' I said quickly, waving in the direction of our cottage, which had sat happily on the edge of Muir Woods for ever such a long time, or

LIBRARY.

even longer.

For a few seconds, Thing seemed

thoughtful and started
rocking from side to
side, muttering its
swishy-swishy song.
'Hey, Thing; what's
with the swish-swish
stuff?' Jackson asked.

'I like sound of swish
word,' it said with what
might have been a hairy

shrug. 'But what *is* swish?'

Thing blinked at us both with its
bushbaby eyes, waiting for our answer.

Me and Jackson blinked back, our minds a
matching blank.

'Boy say, "I swish I not go school
tomorrow!"' Thing tried to explain.

Ah, *now* I got it. We'd been chatting over

the fence as we walked down our gardens to see Thing.

'What Jackson was talking about was a *wish*, not a *swish*. A wish is when you really, really want something. Do you understand?'

'Yes! Yes, *please!*' said Thing, clapping its hands together excitedly. '*I* has a swish!'

'Do you? What is it?' asked Jackson.

'I swish I go to *school*! I *like* to learn!'

Thing looked hopefully up into my face.

Jackson turned and grinned at me.

'No!!' I yelped. 'It would be *way* too dangerous! What if someone saw you, Thing?'

(What if you got upset at something, got all ARRGHH! and landed us in TERRIBLE trouble? I fretted silently.)

'But Ruby, we could smuggle Thing into school in my rucksack!' Jackson blurted. 'It's got a sort of mesh panel in it. So Thing could

stay hidden, but be able to peek through the mesh to see what was going on!!'

'Oh yes, *please*, Rubby?' Thing begged, holding its paws up in front of it. 'Just a once only? I be *good*! And quiet as a snail!'

Jackson took one look at Thing and immediately copied what it was doing, opening his eyes cartoon-wide and holding his hands up like a pleading puppy.

'Pretty please with jelly babies on top, Ruby?' said Jackson, tilting his head to the side.

My brain was yelling no, *no*, NO! very loudly, but I heard my mouth say something completely different.

'Er . . . uh . . . OK, then.'

Oops.

At that point, my brain rolled its eyes and mumbled darkly, 'Don't say I didn't warn you . . .'

Really, truly, seriously

Boys just can't help thwacking things, can they?

If a girl sees something strange on the ground, like a funny-shaped stone, she'll stop and look at it.

The first thing a *boy* will do is hit it with a stick, or kick it really hard, just to see how far it'll go.

'Jackson, honey, it's better not to do that,'

Mum said, as the three of us hurried along the windy country lane towards school. 'You see, birds nest in there and you *could* disturb or hurt them.'

She was saying that stuff because Jackson had just started idly thwacking the hedgerows with his rucksack.

Luckily for Thing, it was in *my* bag, and not *Jackson's*.

(My cerise-pink holdall was shiny and clean, and only had a pencil case in it. Jackson's rucksack was probably stuffed with smelly PE socks and a disintegrating sausage roll from last Tuesday.)

'Oh! Sorry, Mrs Morgan,' Jackson mumbled apologetically to my mum, going as red as the berries that appear on the thwacked hedgerows in the autumn.

Jackson may be a boy, and a big baboon too, but he's not mean. It's just that until

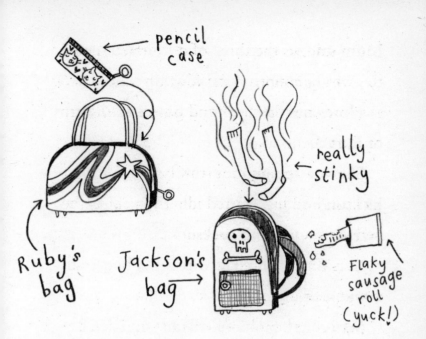

pencil case

Ruby's bag

Jackson's bag →

really stinky

Flaky sausage roll (yuck!)

recently, he'd lived in a big, busy city, and still wasn't used to freaky stuff like fresh air and nature.

'No harm done!' Mum said brightly. 'So how are you two feeling about today?'

EEK!!

I was so stunned by Mum's question that I nearly stopped putting one foot in front of the other.

Jackson was spooked by what she'd said

too – his face had switched from berry-red to huh?-grey in a nano-second.

How could Mum know about Thing and our plan to smuggle it into school today?

'The geography test?' she said, spotting our panicked, puzzled faces. 'Come on – it's surely not going to be *that* bad, guys!'

'Uh, um, uh, no! Yes, I mean!' I bumbled, while Jackson let out a huge sigh.

With my holdall up on my shoulder, I knew that Thing could only see forward, out of a five-centimetre gap where I hadn't done

UM...

the zip right up.

But if it had been able to look left, it would have seen another frown on another forehead – Mum's this time.

'Should we hurry? Let's hurry!' I said quickly, before Mum started asking tricky questions, like why me and Jackson were acting so totally *weird*.

Thankfully, we were coming up to the edge of town, and the school was directly across the road. Spotting the traffic pause at the zebra crossing, I hoicked my bag up higher and ran.

'Wait up, Ruby!' I heard Mum laugh, somewhere behind me. 'It's only ten to – the bell doesn't go for another five minutes!'

Urgh . . . five more minutes of hiding my secret from Mum.

It was making me feel a bit ill, actually.

Having Thing hidden at the bottom of

the garden was risky enough. But knowing Mum and Thing were so close – only separated by a thin bit of dark pink vinyl – well, it was a *hundred* times riskier.

'Are you all right, darling?' said Mum, catching me up, just as we got to the school gate. 'You've been acting a bit strange this morn— Oh! Ruby!! You're not well!'

What?

Mum wasn't looking at my face when she spoke, and neither was Jackson.

They were both staring at the little trail of sick dribbling down the side of my bag, the side with the slightly open zip.

Yuck!

But oh dear . . .

It wasn't *me* who wasn't well, but I knew I'd better start acting like it was.

'Cause if I told Mum that it was actually my pet troll/fairy/squirrel/*thing* that had

been sick, she'd be sure as sure could be that
I was really, truly,
seriously ill . . .

4

Jellified with panic

I knew it was possible to get travel-sick in a
car or a bus or a boat.

I just didn't realise you could get travel-
sick inside a cerise-pink holdall.

'It very, very bumpy, Rubby,' Thing said
sorrowfully. 'Very, very, very, very, *very*
bumpy . . .'

'Poor you!' I murmured, dipping a tissue
into the glass of water next to my bed and
dabbing it on Thing's face. 'There . . . is that

nice and cool?'

Thing was flopped on top of my duvet
like a half-filled hot-water bottle, its head
resting on the pillow.

My cat Christine was licking Thing's
tummy fur comfortingly.

My holdall was dumped at the end of my bed, whiffing a bit.

'*Yes*, nice and *cool*, please . . .' Thing purred, all limp and feeble.

'Well, once you feel better, I'll open the window and you can escape down the wisteria.'

Thing blinked at me for a second or two.

Hadn't it understood what I'd just said?

Or was it just studying my nose?

'What is meaning of whispery-*ahh* . . ., Rubby?' it asked.

(OK, so it *hadn't* understood me.)

'No, it's not whispery-*ahh* . . . it's wis-*ter*-i-*a*. It's the big plant growing up the side of the house,' I explained. '*You* called it tangle-vine once before.'

'Ah, yes, please,' Thing said with small nod. 'So when my tummy not feeling spinny-spinny, I go climb down wistery-*ahh* . . .'

'Um, yes. But just rest for now.' I nodded too, quite proud of my Florence Nightingale skills.

Not to mention my acting skills. Back at the school gates, I'd managed to convince Mum that I had come over all woozy.

She'd taken one look at me, turned me right around, and marched me straight back home, which felt . . .

- strange (I don't like missing school), but

- good (the closer I'd got to school, the more I was thinking it was a VBI - **VERY BAD IDEA** - to take Thing there after all).

'Rubby?'

'Yes, Thing?' I answered, gently stroking its quivery, squirrelly ears.

'*Why* you have small furs up your nose?'

(OK, so it *had* been studying my nose just now.)

'It's not fur, it's hair,' I told it, as I got up off the bed and went to grab a book I'd just spotted on one of my shelves. 'You've probably got them too.'

I wriggled the book free from a pile of other dusty-looking books and walked back to the bed. I was just in time to spot Thing pressing its own wet, black snout, piggy style.

'No, thank you. All my fur on *outside*. What is book, Rubby?'

I flopped down next to Thing, and opened the first page of *My First Day at School!*

A picture book called *My First Day at School!* probably isn't something you should

still have when you are nine years old like me. The trouble is, I find it very hard to chuck useless things away. (Maybe that's why I'm friends with Jackson – ha!)

This book was a good example. I might not have opened a page of it since I was three, but now it was going to come in handy as a way of teaching Thing all about school, without it ever having to step inside a classroom.

With our little and large heads touching, I began.

'Right. Today I am going to give you a lesson ab—'

THUNK.

Squeak!!

CLUNK!!

'Here we go, Ruby! I've made you some honey tea and a bit of toast,' Mum chattered, juggling a tray as she wrestled with my door handle and breezed into my bedroom.

EEK!!

I sat bolt upright and wondered if I really *was* going to be sick.

Help – Mum was going to take one look at the slightly alien-looking woodland creature on my bed and freak!

It was bound to happen any second now ...

'I only put margarine on the toast because I thought peanut butter might be too rich for your funny tummy,' Mum chattered on, putting the tray down on my bedside cabinet.

Any second now . . .

'Phew! Something tells me that bag will need a good wash!' Mum muttered, turning her attention to the holdall at the bottom of the bed. 'How did you manage to be sick *inside* it, Ruby?!'

'Uh, yes . . . no . . . I don't know,' I fumbled, only really hearing the thumpa-dumping of my heart and some insanely loud purring coming from Christine cat.

OK, any second now . . .

'What? Oh, never mind. Ruby, try to drink some of your tea while it's still nice and warm – oh!'

See? She'd finally spotted Thing, hadn't she?!

Hadn't she?

'You know something? You're really *very* pale, Ruby!' Mum said with a frown that Thing would find most impressive.

Not that I was about to turn around and see if it was looking, of course.

I didn't dare move, or think or *hope* – all I could do was stay statue-still, while Mum put a hand on my forehead and felt for a fever.

Phew; she thought I was ill, not just jellified with panic, right?

But *that* wouldn't last.

Mum was so close to me, so close to the bed, that there was just no *way* she could miss Thing!

'Hmm. You don't *feel* that hot,' Mum yakked away. 'Tell you what, I'll go and get the thermometer, just to be on the safe side.'

I *think* it's in the First Aid box in the kitchen. Just you sip your tea while I go and look.'

And with that she wandered out of my room, taking my whiffy holdall with her.

Thud! Thud! Thud! went Mum's feet on the stairs.

Huh? What? Where?! went my head as I spun around – and saw absolutely *nothing* on the bed except Christine cat!

'Thing?' I whispered, glancing around for it.

'Mrrrr . . . *yew*!'

That noise; it sounded a bit like a faraway kitten in distress. It certainly hadn't anything to do with Christine, 'cause she was all curled up in a purry circle, doing what she does best (sleeping).

'*Thing!*' I whispered again, even though I could hear Mum safely clattering cupboard doors in the kitchen down below. 'Where *are* you?'

'Help!' came a voice so tiny it could have come from a visiting bed-bug.

'Is that you?' I said stupidly, trying to figure out the direction the voice was coming from.

'Rubby, *help!*' the tiny, muffled voice called out again. 'Not – not *breathe!*'

It was then that I spotted a pair of triangular, fluffy red wings on Christine's back.

Wait a minute; they weren't wings . . . they were squirrelly ears, attached to something *underneath* her.

And those ears were twirling and twitching in a most peculiar way.

In class a while back, we learned about Morse code, where you wave in different ways and it means stuff. If I could read what those ears were trying to say now, I was pretty certain it would be, 'SOS! I AM

BEING ACCIDENTALLY SMOTHERED
BY AN ELDERLY CAT!'

'Thing – hold on!' I gasped, scooping a
startled Christine up from her comfy sleeping
spot and plopping her further down the bed.

'Peh!' sneezed Thing, brushing cat hairs
from its snout.

'Are you OK?' I asked it, helping it upright.

'Yes, please,' it spluttered. 'I not know cat
words so good. I say "too heavy, please", but
Chriss–cat not understanding . . .'

'Mainly because she was too busy

snoozing!' I muttered, while tsk-ing at
Christine.

'Don't be **ARRGHH!**, Rubby. Cat *nice*
cat. Hide me good!'

'Yeah, nearly hid you to *death*,' I sighed.
'But listen, I think we'd better get you out of
here, 'cause Mum'll be back in a second. Are
you OK to climb down to the garden now?'

'Yes, *please*,' said Thing slightly woozily, as
I carried it over to the window. 'But Rubby,
I still swish I got to be at school today! I *sad*.
You sad, Rubby?'

'Yes,' I lied to be kind.

Nope, I'm glad, I said silently to myself,
opening the window so Thing could scamper
off down the whispery-*ahh* ...

Listening as it **plumpf**-ed and **ploomf**-ed its
way downwards, I thought of a swish of my
own.

I swished I was sitting next to Jackson

Miller right now.

'Cause after faking illness and having my head melt with stress, doing a lovely, boring geography test sounded *much* more fun . . .

Project
Stowaway

It was a normal Wednesday lunchtime.

Almost.

Here's what was normal about it:

- I was in the queue in the dinner hall

- I was being shouted at by Mrs Sweeney the dinner lady

'Could I just have the sweetcorn and cucumber, and no lettuce, please?'

(That was me. I'm not a big fan of lettuce.)

'Absolutely *not*! Salad comes WITH lettuce! I expect you to *eat* it!!'

(That was Mrs Sweeney the dinner lady, who is not a big fan of children.)

Now I suppose I should tell you what *wasn't* normal about this Wednesday lunchtime. There were two reasons it was odd:

- I was wearing a blue, fluffy, fleecy zip-up top that was far too warm for the time of year

- The zip of the fleece was being pulled down - **FROM THE INSIDE** ...

'Thank you,' I mumbled quickly, taking my jacket potato and unwanted lettuce and hurrying away from Mrs Sweeney's gaze before she spotted the weirdness going on in the region of my chest.

'Oi!'

Uh-oh – that was Mrs Sweeney, and she seemed to be 'oi'ing at *me*.

'Yes?' I said, turning back around, and holding my tray up to hide the faint rummaging I could feel going on.

'*No* coats and jackets in the dinner hall! It's *against* the *rules*! Get it off!! NOW!!' she barked, waving salad tongs at me menacingly.

'Oh, it's *not* a coat or a jacket! It's a fleece!' I gabbled, hurrying away from Mrs Sweeney and her growls and glares.

My teacher Miss Wilson had been a bit confused by my fleece this morning.

But when I explained that I was still feeling a little shivery after my 'illness' the day before she'd said, 'Well, OK, then, fine,' in that way teachers do when they don't quite believe you but can't prove you're fibbing.

'Ruby!'

Ah, there was Jackson – he'd grabbed the small table that no one ever likes to sit at, because it's right next to the boys' toilet. Perfect.

'The cook and the other dinner ladies are all right,' Jackson said, nodding back towards the serving counter as I sat down next to him. 'But Mrs Sweeney is *such* a total grouch, isn't she?'

'Yes, *please*,' agreed my chest.

OK, it was Thing, who was nestled in the deep, inside left pocket of my overly cosy fleece.

It was lucky that me and Jackson (and

Thing) were at a table on our own, and that I'd chosen the seat facing the wall. 'Cause if we'd been sharing one of the normal, bigger, busier tables, other kids might have heard Thing's purry voice or seen that my zip was on its way down *again*, as if by magic.

'Thing!' I hissed. 'What are you doing? Do you *want* to get caught?!'

'I just very, very hot in here, Rubby,' it whispered back. 'Very, very, very, very, *very* hot!'

'*Tell* me about it!' I whinged, pulling at the zip a bit myself and fanning a serviette in the direction of Thing.

'Don't get grumpy just 'cause of meanie Sweeney!' Jackson joked, pulling a stupid face that I think was meant to look like the dinner lady.

I'd have laughed, only I was grumpy with him too.

'I shouldn't have let you two persuade me to do this!' I said in a snippy voice, at the same time slipping my glass of water inside my fleece.

Thing gazed up at me as it scrabbled for the straw.

'But I been good, Rubby! *So* quiet! Just listeninging!'

'Shush!' I told it.

It didn't matter that this morning had gone well.

It didn't matter that Thing had huddled
patiently in the depths of the hideaway
pocket all through literacy and numeracy
and break time and history.

What mattered was that I'd taken an
awful risk
bringing Thing
here, and all
because of a
homemade sick-
bag.

'Aww! *Look*
what it made!'
Jackson had cooed this morning, pointing to
Thing and the fabric conditioner bottle top
it was clutching.

'Maybe I hold *this* on way to school, so
I not make a *mess* again, Rubby?' it had
purred hopefully.

Big softie that I am, I instantly melted.

I even came up with the idea of Thing travelling inside my fleece, which I figured wouldn't be so bouncy and spinny-spinny as my holdall.

So maybe the person I should be *most* grumpy with was *me* . . .

'Hey, what's been your favourite thing about school so far?' I heard Jackson saying, and immediately got *extra* grumpy with him.

'Jackson! What will people *think*?! It looks like you're talking to my polo shirt!!' I told him off, feeling my cheeks go pink.

'OK! OK!' sighed Jackson. 'Chill out! I'm just asking Thing a simple question!'

'I like flushy-flush box,' came a mutter from deep inside my fleece.

I knew Thing was talking about our visit to the girls' toilets at break time.

But as far as I was concerned, it wasn't the time or place to chat about the wonders of weeing, even if the cubicle and the flushing toilet in it was as exciting for Thing as fireworks night and a rollercoaster rolled into one.

'Well, save your questions for home-time!' I told Jackson, knowing that I sounded like Miss Wilson again. ''Cause we can't take any chances! We can't let *anyone* find out about Thing!'

'Honestly, Rubby! You worry too much!' Jackson grinned at me annoyingly. 'Hiding Thing has worked fine. What could go wrong?'

Well, we might have got away with Project Stowaway so far, but I worried that Jackson saying 'What could go wrong?' would put an instant jinx on us.

And sure enough, at just after three o'clock that afternoon, something went very, very, very, very, *very* wrong indeed.

Jinx!

Sssnnnuuuzzz!
Mneeeee . . .

The time: 2.59 p.m. on Wednesday afternoon (i.e. one minute till all the wrong-ness started).

'Dear me, Ruby!' Miss Wilson gasped. 'Your cheeks are like two tomatoes, they're so red!'

My cheeks actually felt like two tomatoes that were *on fire*.

In fact, my whole body felt like a radiator that had been turned up full blast.

I remember a newsreader once talking
about holidaymakers in Spain or Greece or
somewhere collapsing 'cause of a heatwave.
I felt like I was about to pass out through
heat exhaustion in the third row of the ICT
room.

'Ruby, you've had that fleece on *all* day,'
said Miss Wilson. 'But you can't possibly
need it on now – not with the hot air these

computers generate! *Please* take it off . . .'

'Yes, Miss Wilson,' I muttered weakly, glad to finally escape from what was beginning to feel like a zip-up duvet.

There was only about quarter of an hour to go before the end-of-day bell, and Thing would be safe enough dangling from the back of my chair for a few (deliciously cool) minutes.

Like Jackson said, what could possibly go wrong . . . ?

Miss Wilson watched, puzzled, as I wriggled out of my sleeves in slow motion, and hung the fleecy evvvvvver-sooooo-*gennnnntly* on the back of my chair.

'You can have a drink, if you'd like,' she said, pointing to the bulge on the drooping left-hand side of the fleece.

She'd noticed the Thing-shaped lump for the first time after lunch (I'd forgotten to keep my arms across my chest to cover it up). When she asked me what was in there, Jackson had a brainwave and shouted 'A WATER BOTTLE!', which was pretty quick thinking, even if it *was* a bit loud.

'In a little while,' I replied, hoping Miss Wilson didn't insist.

I know Thing could be mistaken for a comfy cat cushion, but I didn't suppose anyone would believe it was a novelty water bottle. They don't often come with fur. Or eyes. Or twitchy, squirrelly ears.

'It'll be OK,' Jackson leant over and muttered to me now, which made me want to punch the big baboon in the arm.

That's 'cause he was *pointing at the Thing-shaped lump as he spoke.*

How much of a giveaway was that?!?

'Quiet, everyone!' Miss Wilson said
to, well, *everyone*, even though she was
particularly looking at Jackson. 'I want your
projects finished by the end of the lesson. So
let's have ABSOLUTE silence and your *best*
concentration, please!'

Doing as I was told, I stared at my
computer screen and carried on with
the coastal erosion diagrams we were all
supposed to be designing for our geography
project.

Actually, I got quite into it. All that coastal
erosion was very soothing. For the first time
all day, it was as if I'd finally forgotten to
be nervous or scared or stressed about the
stowaway in my fleece.

That feeling lasted for . . . oooh, about
three whole minutes, till the funny snoring
started.

'**S**ss**hhhhhh**υυυυ**zzzzzzz**! **M**neeee . . .

Sss**hhhhhh**υυυυ**zzzzzzz**! **M**neeee . . .

Sss**hhhhhh**υυυυ**zzzzzzz**! **M**neeee . . .'

Somebody somewhere in the ICT room sniggered. Which was followed by a few titters, and a smattering of giggles.

I flipped my head round to face Jackson, and Jackson flipped his head around to face me.

Then we both dropped our gaze down towards the gently vibrating fleece on the back of my chair.

'*Who* is making that silly noise?' Miss Wilson suddenly announced.

EEK!!

What were we going to do?

Luckily, Jackson had a plan.

Unluckily, it was going to make our teacher pretty angry with him.

'It was me, Miss Wilson!' my dumb but

brave friend announced, shooting his hand straight up.

'Well, Jackson, I know you like to play the clown, but—'

Straightaway, I saw that this was my chance to smuggle the *real* snorer out.

'Er, Miss Wilson!' I interrupted, jumping up from my seat and grabbing my heavy fleece. 'I feel like I might be sick again . . . can I be excused, please?'

Miss Wilson waved me away, before turning back to Jackson with a face as grumpy as a wasp in a jar.

'Peh! Oof! Eeep!' came several tiny muffled noises as I bundled the fleece in my arms and bolted for the girls' loos.

Once I was safely locked in a cubicle and sitting on the closed lid of the toilet seat, I loosened my grip, and unrolled a fuzzily crumpled Thing out on to my lap.

'Rubby!?' it squeaked. 'We in flushy-flush box! *Why* is here?'

'You fell asleep in the last lesson, and started *snoring*,' I told it. 'I *had* to get you out of class quick!'

Thing's humongous eyes widened.

'Peh! I hear teacher yak-yakking at you, Rubby,' Thing bumbled. 'But then room very, very hot. I very, very, very, very, *very* tired and—'

'Look, I *understand* why you fell asleep,

Thing. But you've got Jackson into a lot of trouble! He took the blame when you started snoring, and Miss Wilson has probably sent him to the Head's office!!'

Thing sat hunched apologetically on my knees, blinking madly.

'Is that a kind of *wood*, Rubby?'

'No! The Head's office is *not* a kind of wood, Thing!' I snapped. 'The Head Teacher is the most important person in the school. And I bet he's shouting at poor Jackson right now!'

Thing's eyes grew even *wider*, even though I didn't think that was physically possible.

'But Rubby . . . boy my *friend*!' Thing purred, anxiously rocking from side to side. 'I *bad* thing. I very, very bad thing. I very, very, very, *very* bad thing!'

It was on the fourth or fifth 'very' that I felt a familiar tremble.

Uh-oh.

A tremble happened whenever Thing was feeling angry or upset or generally ARRGHH!.

And once Thing felt ARRGHH!, strange stuff always happened.

Strange *magical* stuff.

(Magical stuff that is a bit strange, actually.)

'Hey, you know something? Now I think about it, I'm *sure* Jackson will be fine!' I said hurriedly, wishing I hadn't made it all sound so terrible and important.

But Thing kept right on trembling. I crossed my fingers and made a quick swish that it would stop.

'Honestly! I mean, I bet you he *hasn't* been sent to the Head *after* all!' I babbled on. 'I bet Miss Wilson thought the snoring was really cute and funny, and the whole class is laughing about it!'

Nice try, but it was too late. The seriously spectacular weirdness was already starting . . .

CRACKLE
SPIT
FIZZZZzzZ!!

Flickers of light danced around the toilet cubicle.

Sparkles cartwheeled around my head.

And then just as soon as the mini fireworks show started, it stopped.

'Thing – what did you do?' I asked, uncrossing my useless fingers and glancing around the small space. All I could see was the same cream plastic walls, the same white cubicle door, the same square grey floor tiles.

'Not know, Rubby!' it mumbled sheepishly, twisting its tiny hands together.

Doof!

I jumped. There'd been the softest little thump under my bottom, as if someone had knocked on the underside of the toilet lid I was sitting on.

Gulp.

I stood up, scooping Thing into my arms, and stared down at the closed toilet seat.

Did I dare flip up the lid to see what had *doof*-ed?

Before I could get myself in a tangle of 'Will I? Won't I?'s, I shot my arm out.

And with a flick of the wrist, I discovered

. . . that the loo was filled to the *brim* with cherry tomatoes!

'Thing!!' I gasped. 'Why are there so many tomatoes in the toilet?'

As soon as I said that I remembered Miss Wilson talking about my cheeks being tomato-red. Had Thing heard that just before it fell asleep?

'I get in big muddle, Rubby!' it said all alarmed, clinging onto me like a strange hairy baby.

'All right, but how are we going to get *rid* of them?' I fretted, aware that the bell would be ringing soon and I needed to get back to class.

Thing blinked fast before suggesting something.

'Flushy-flush?'

I gazed down at the mounds of cherry tomatoes, and knew *that* wasn't going to work.

'I've got a better idea,' I said, picking up my fleece with one hand and nudging Thing to clamber back into the hideaway pocket. 'We'll run away and pretend it's got nothing to do with us!'

Pulling on the lop-sided fleece, I hurried out of the girls' toilets and back along the corridor.

The poor school cleaner – *she'd* be the one who'd have to sort out the great tomato mystery.

What would she think had happened?

Maybe she'd suspect that all the tomato-haters at school had got extra helpings from meanie Sweeney and dumped them in the loo together.

Hey, it wasn't *such* a mad idea.

It once took me six or seven flushes to get rid of all the lettuce leaves . . .

7

Another VBI

Hurray!

It was Thursday morning, and I was heading off to school feeling absolutely *great*.

My cerise-pink holdall was shiny and clean and had nothing in it apart from a hairbrush, some pens and half a packet of chewy mints.

I was wearing my school skirt and shirt, plus a thin blue cardie tied tight around my waist, all with absolutely *no* large pockets to hide anything in.

It was Jackson's dad's turn to walk us to school, and as I wandered next door to meet Jackson and Mr Miller, I knew that Thing was happily snuffling about in the trees at the bottom of the garden, doing whatever Thing liked to do.

Best of all, with Thing safe at home, it meant there'd be no tomatoes in the toilet or other magical mishaps to worry about at school today.

Wasn't that ordinary and boring and brilliant?

('*Promise* we're never, *ever* going to do that again!' I'd said, once the three of us arrived safely home from school yesterday. Jackson promised. Thing just looked confused and said, 'What is promise *meaning*, Rubby?')

'Well, hi, there, Ruby! Would madam like a lift to school?' Mr Miller joked, as I turned into his driveway.

He was holding open the passenger door of his big red car and bowing low.

'Aren't we walking today?' I asked, gazing up at the extremely sunny sun.

As there wasn't a hailstone or a tornado on the horizon, I expected Mr Miller to say that he had to go straight off to a meeting afterwards or something.

'It's Jackson's fault – he can't walk very far,' said Mr Miller. 'He seems to have pulled a muscle in his calf.'

At that second, I saw Jackson step out of his front door with two very healthy-looking legs.

But as soon as he saw me, his right leg seemed to take a turn for the worse.

'What did you do?' I called over to him, as he began limping towards the car.

'I sort of *twisted* it.'

'How?' I asked.

Jackson squirmed.

'When I was ... uh ... brushing my teeth.'

Huh?

What kind of lame fiberoonie was *that*?

Jackson was covering up for something for sure!

Had he hurt it doing something *embarrassing*?

Like dancing when he was putting his boxer shorts on and falling flat on his face?

(His bedroom window was right opposite mine. I'd once seen him singing along to loud hip-hop wearing nothing but Bart Simpson boxers. It was enough to give a girl nightmares for *weeks* ...)

'What's he like, eh, Ruby?' Mr Miller laughed, as he climbed into the driver's seat.

A donut crossed with a big baboon, I thought.

Still, I should be kind and considerate. After all, Jackson had had to put up with

a *monster* telling-off from Miss Wilson yesterday for 'snoring', AND he wasn't allowed out at break times for the rest of the week as punishment.

'Do you want to go in the front?' I offered him, knowing EVERYONE prefers to sit there if they have a choice.

'Uh ... no – it's all right. *You* can have it.'

That was very generous of Jackson. He wasn't *usually* so generous.

I hesitated, wondering if he'd maybe put a whoopee cushion in the passenger seat ...

Nope, nothing there.

'Er, thanks,' I said warily, as I got into the car, and heard the back door clunk shut.

'So, how's school treating you, Ruby?' Mr Miller began chatting.

Mr Miller must have a degree in chatting, as he is very good at it. He can chatter endlessly about everything, and all you have to do is say, 'yes', 'no' and 'fine, thanks' in between his bouts of chatting.

'How slow is this farmer going, eh?' Mr Miller grumbled chattily, as we got stuck behind a tractor on the country lane that wended and wound its way towards school.

'Yes', 'no' and 'fine, thanks' didn't seem to work as answers all of a sudden, so I just 'mmmm!'ed.

Still, since Mr Miller was craning his neck to see the road ahead, I took the chance to peek round at Jackson, who'd been spookily quiet.

I mean, if his dad has a degree in chatting, then Jackson should have one for talking rubbish, so it felt kind of *eerie*, him being so silent . . .

'You OK?' I mouthed at him, so his dad
didn't suspect that something was up.

'Yeah!' he mouthed back.

But he didn't *seem* OK.

He was sitting completely stiff and
straight, his eyes wide, his rucksack perched
neatly on his lap.

That was a perfectly good look for any
other kid, but for Jackson it was all wrong.

The 'normal' Jackson didn't so much sit as

slouch. And in the mornings, it took him till at least half-nine for his eyes to be properly awake and more than half-open.

'Right! Should be able to overtake at last, if I put my foot down!' Mr Miller announced, swerving the car suddenly and accelerating to the speed of light.

'**EEK!**' came a small sound of alarm from somewhere in the vicinity of the back seat.

As soon as the G-force would let me, I turned around and scowled at Jackson.

'What?' he mouthed, trying his best to look innocent.

But I knew right then that he was hiding a guilty secret in his rucksack.

It looked as if he'd . . .

- forgotten his promise, and

- had a **VBI**, or

- had a **VBII** – a very bad idea **INDEED**.

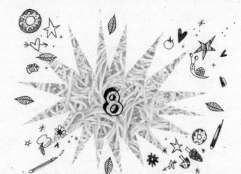

Spot the donut

'Are you really thick, or just a bit mad?'

It was a question I'd been dying to ask Jackson for more than an hour and a half.

After getting stuck behind the tractor, we were only *just* in time for school. The Head Teacher was hustling everyone inside in one great, big, bundled rush, and I lost sight of Jackson.

Then in class, I'd forgotten the other year-group class were crowding in with us for the first lesson, to watch a film about rainforests.

Then straight after *that* we had art, but I wasn't in Jackson's group.

All I could do was shoot him a what-are-you-playing-at? scowl across the paint pots, while keeping an eye on the motionless black rucksack lurking under his desk.

In fact, it took me all the way to break time to get a chance to ask it, and to get Jackson's useless answer.

'I'm not thick *or* mad!' Jackson protested, talking to me through the slightly open window of the classroom, where he was doing his detention for snoring.

'So you think it's completely clever and sensible to smuggle Thing in here again today?' I whispered, so no one could overhear me.

Though no one was listening – the playground was full of school-kid whoops, high-pitched nattering and roars.

'Look, I snuck down to the trees to see Thing this morning,' Jackson began his explanation, 'and it was asking what we'd do at school today.'

'So?' I shrugged.

'So I told it we were going to watch a telly programme about rainforests as part of our geography topic,' he carried on. 'Thing got all excited about the word "forest", and was absolutely *desperate* to see the film. What could I do?'

'You could've said *no*!' I growled, thinking of the note that was taped up in the girls' toilets this morning:

Any pranks taking place in here will be treated with the utmost seriousness!

Gulp. The tomatoes had been discovered, then!

'See – I guessed you'd be mad at me, Ruby. *That's* why I didn't tell you.'

'Well, you guessed right. And *I'm* guessing that you made up the excuse about having a sore leg?'

'Uh, yeah.'

'Just so you could get your dad to give us a lift?'

'Uh, yeah.'

''Cause you thought that would get Thing to school quicker, so it wouldn't be sick in your bag like it was in mine?'

'Uh . . . yeah. But Dad drove too fast and it was *still* sick,' Jackson admitted, giving me a goofy, big baboon smile, as though that would make me forgive him. 'I had to clean out Thing's fabric conditioner top in the sink just now!'

'Oh, Jackson!' I sighed.

I'd *just* spotted something pretty disastrous.

'But today's the last time *ever*, Ruby!' Jackson tried to reassure me, not realising what was going on behind his back. 'I *told* Thing that. *And* I told it to behave today. So everything's totally cool.'

'You're one hundred per cent sure about that?' I challenged him.

'Absolutely! Scout's honour!' Jackson promised.

But we all know how useless Jackson's promises are, don't we?

'So Miss Wilson is going to be OK about what Thing is doing right now?' I asked, pointing at the group of tables where the paints and brushes were stacked, ready to go back in the cupboard after break.

Thing was holding a squeezy plastic bottle of yellow paint in one paw, and a bottle

of red paint in the other, and was *paddling*
in the great gloops of colour oozing out of
them both.

'*Nooooo!*' yelped Jackson, whirling away
from me and over towards Thing, who was
now waddling over Miss Wilson's plastic
folder of notes.

Of course I thought Jackson was the
biggest donut in the history of cream

cakes for smuggling Thing to school again.

But I wasn't a meanie (like Mrs Sweeney) and *of course* I couldn't just stand there and let Thing be discovered and Jackson get break-time detention for life.

And so just a few seconds later, I'd snuck myself *back* into school to begin the big tidy-up.

'Rubby! It so exciting! I see *forest* on VT!'

'TV!' I corrected it, wiping red + yellow = orange footprints off Mrs Wilson's folder.

'That forest has birdies and buzzies not in *my* forest!'

Well, yes. I'd gone for walks in Muir Woods since I was little and never seen any toucans or tarantulas.

'Thing, can you get back into the rucksack?' Jackson urged it, trying to stop it walking paint across things it shouldn't, like Miss Wilson's folder (again) and the remote control for the overhead projector.

'I like little furry "eeek! eeek! eeek!" best,' Thing burbled on, so thrilled by the rainforest programme that it couldn't contain itself. 'What animal *is* little furry "eeek! eek! eek!", boy?'

'It was a tamarin monkey,' Jackson replied. 'Can you get in my bag now?'

'I *like* tammy monkey!' Thing jabbered on. 'I not *like* long thing. What *is* long thing, boy?'

'It was a snake,' said Jackson. 'Now can you—'

'I not *like* snake,' Thing muttered darkly. 'I know what it say!'

'What did it say?' I asked, grabbing Thing up and attempting to wipe its feet clean with a paper towel.

No matter how much of a rush and a mess we were in, I couldn't resist knowing what an Amazonian snake had to say for itself.

'Snake say, "Mmm, I think I *eat* little tammy monkey!"'

I pulled a face, partly because of what Thing had just said, and partly because Thing was covered in more paint than I had realised.

'How are we going to clean you up?' I sighed.

'Maybe put me in flushy-flush?' Thing said brightly.

'Don't tempt me . . .' I muttered, rubbing harder.

'Here,' said Jackson, holding up the wastepaper bin with one hand and the rucksack with the other. 'The end-of-break bell is just about to go!'

Urgh! The whole class would come jumbling in any second now. At top speed, I dropped the furball in the bag and the scrunched paper towel in the bin.

'OK. Now *promise* me,' I said, staring hard at Thing as it peered through the mesh panel of the rucksack, 'you will not *move*, or *snore*, or get into *any* trouble, or do *any* magic for the rest of the day!!'

Thing's tiny claws hooked through the lattice of the mesh, and I could just make out that it was nodding at me.

'I not doing any of those *not* things,' it purred. 'I *promising*, Rubby.'

Sadly, it turned out that Thing was as lousy at keeping promises as Jackson Donut Miller . . .

92

Tramplings and boings

A dark storm-cloud hovered over us.

Which was strange, because we were
sitting in the brightly lit dinner hall.

'*What*,' bellowed the dark storm-cloud, 'is
THIS!'

The dark storm-cloud was wearing a
white pinafore and matching hat and a
name badge that read '*Mrs Sweeney, Catering
Assistant*'.

'It's ... uh ... some noodles?' I mumbled,

wondering why exactly Mrs Sweeney
was pointing at my plate, and why it was
annoying her so much.

'*What*,' Mrs Sweeney bellowed some more,
'is *wrong* with them?'

I glanced down again at the wiggly
wodge of uneaten noodles.

The stress of keeping Thing undercover
had messed with my appetite, I guess.

Then again, the noodles were particularly
disgusting today. The cook had boiled them
so much they'd practically turned into gluey
mush. (*Not* my favourite lunch.)

'Er, nothing,' I mumbled. 'I'm just not very
hungry today!'

'*What a WASTE!*' Mrs Sweeney tsk-ed
fiercely, making me feel as if I was
personally responsible for all the starving
children in the world.

Phew; she seemed about to stomp off . . .

but then found something *else* to moan
about.

'*You!*' she barked at Jackson.

Jackson jumped in his seat, then checked
his own plate for wrongness.

But apart from a stray pea, there was nothing on it. He was much too greedy to let a little thing like worry put him off his food.

'*Rules!!*' snarled Mrs Sweeney, flicking her tea towel at the sign on the wall behind us. '*What* does number FIVE say?!?'

'It, uh . . .' Jackson fumbled, 'it says, "*Keep bags off the tables and chairs*".'

'So you *can* read, then?! Well, how about doing like it says and putting your bag on the floor! *NOW!!*'

Mrs Sweeney lunged forward, as if she was going to remove the offending rucksack herself.

But Jackson beat her to it and grabbed his bag and its delicate contents before meanie Sweeney had a chance to cause Thing any lasting damage.

'We were leaving anyway!' Jackson

mumbled, and screeched back his chair.

I followed him quickly, noticing that we were just about the last people in here. All the other kids had already disappeared into the sunshine of the playground.

And most of the dinner hall staff had stomped off to the steaminess of the kitchen, laden with mountains of dirty dishes.

BRINGGGGGGG!!! the end-of-lunch bell suddenly deafened us.

'Where are you going?' I asked Jackson, as soon as we were outside. It looked like he'd been about to head off to the main school building, instead of the gym hall, which was just across the way.

'Oh! I forgot it was PE today!' he said, happily.

Looking this way and that, he checked no one was around before hoisting his bag up to his face.

'Hey, Thing!' he muttered directly to it. 'You'll like watching us do PE! At the beginning, we get to go on a big bouncy square called a *trampoline*. When it's *my* turn, I'm going to pretend I'm jumping on meanie Sweeney's *head* . . .'

'Trampling,' repeated a tiny purry voice from inside the bag. I could just see a glint of big eyes and a wet black snout through the mesh section.

'Shhhh!!' I told both Jackson and Thing.

After just a few strides, we were already at the gym building, and needed to concentrate.

'Shhhh!' repeated the little purry voice, always on the lookout for new words to learn.

'Ruby means "be quiet",' Jackson told his bag.

'Jackson – I'm shushing *you* too!' I whispered in a warning voice, as we went inside to join Miss Wilson and the rest of our class.

Speaking of sounds, one I was sure Thing would like was the **boing . . . !! boing . . . !! boing . . . !!** of the trampoline.

Me and Jackson were last in line, but once it was finally my go, I glanced over at the row of benches piled with clothes and bags and quickly picked out Jackson's black rucksack. I pictured our funny little pet Thing peering out through the mesh and '**Boingy . . . boingy . . . boing!!**'ing happily to itself.

For a second, that made me smile, instead of stressing.

But with the very next boing, I was stressing again.

That's because when I was on the upward part of my boing, I got a clear view *out* of the gym window, directly *into* the brightly lit dinner hall.

Which meant I got a clear view of what was going on in there!

'Jackson!' I hissed, still jumping, but waving for him to clamber up and join me.

He frowned, then glanced over at the far end of the gym, where Miss Wilson was handing out hula-hoops to everyone who'd finished warming up on the trampoline.

Once he was sure our teacher was distracted, Jackson leapt on board. We were only supposed to go on the trampoline one at a time, but he could probably tell by the look on my face that it was worth the risk of (another) telling-off.

Boing!!

'What's wrong?' he asked, timing his jumps so we were bouncing together.

Boing!!

'Look!'

Boing!!

'At what?'

Boing!!

'The dining hall! Something –'

Boing!!

'– REALLY weird is going on in there!'

Boing!

'Oh, wow! Oh, *no!*' gasped Jackson, suddenly feeling the same wave of dread that I'd just had a just a second ago, when I caught sight of Mrs Sweeney.

At first glance, I thought she was tangoing as she tidied.

At *second* glance, it seemed like she was pogoing with the plates.

At *third* glance, I realised she was going demented, not dancing, and that a whole twisty tangle of giant noodles was snaking around her and chasing her around the room!

Boing!!

'Thing,' I said breathlessly, 'must have cast a spell on her –'

Boing!!

'– 'cause it heard her being so *rude* to us!'

Boing!!

'But wouldn't we have seen something?
Like –'

Boing!!

'– those sparkles that always happen?'

Boing!!

Before I could answer Jackson, we both
heard a familiar purry voice.

'Boing!'

Me and Jackson stared down, only to see a

small furry creature bouncing and boinging
and falling happily at our feet.

'Hee hee! I *like* trampling!'

EEK!!

It's very hard to stop dead on a
trampoline, but we did our best, sort of
crumpling to our knees and collapsing on
the elasticised canvas.

'Hide it!' I hissed at Jackson, who'd already
grabbed Thing and stuffed it up his T-shirt. 'I'll
go and tell Miss Wilson you feel ill, and that
I'm taking you to the sick-room!!'

It was pretty good as nano-second plans go, but I had no time to feel pleased with myself.

While Jackson clutched his stomach, I rushed through the whirl of hula-hoopers to Miss Wilson.

In a gabbled bumble of words, I told her that I was *sure* Jackson must have the same tummy bug I'd had on Tuesday (yes – the *imaginary* tummy bug!!).

Then I hurriedly told her not to worry when it looked like she might go over and check on him. (Thank goodness for twenty-eight hula-hooping kids who Miss Wilson couldn't leave alone, in case they got in a tangle, probably.)

OK, so it was time to escape! And, er, try to do something about the disaster in the dining room . . .

'Right – let's go,' I hissed at Jackson,

grabbing his rucksack off the bench and rushing us both out of the gym doors.

'But I don't understand – why didn't we feel Thing trembling? It *always* does that right before the magic starts!' said Jackson, as we jogged across the playground.

'Thing was hidden away in here, remember?' I said, holding the black bag up and shaking it a little as we ran.

But with the shaking came an ever-so-familiar FIZZing sound, and *out* rolled a tumble of cartwheeling sparkles!

Well, I guess that answered our *next* question; the mini fireworks show had happened *inside* the rucksack . . .

'Whatever,' Jackson panted, still holding tight to Thing under his T-shirt, as if he was cradling a baby bump.

'But how are we going to fix this?'

'I have NO idea,' I answered, as we hurtled in the dining room, and saw the strange sight of Mrs Sweeney, tied to a chair by living, wibbling ropes of pasta.

Even her mouth was covered by twists and loops of noodles, so her shrieks of alarm sounded more like muffled huffing.

So how come none of dining room staff had come rushing to Mrs Sweeney's rescue?

Well, it was pretty easy to figure out why.

Behind the closed doors that led to the kitchen came the sounds of a radio blaring, people laughing, singing and chatting, the din of pots and pans clattering in the sink and the deep rumble-grumbling of dishwashers.

No wonder the rest of the catering staff didn't know what terrible, noodly fate had befallen Mrs Sweeney.

(And maybe none of them *cared*, since they sounded like they were having fun, and fun wasn't something that Mrs Sweeney was particularly into, by the looks of it.)

So . . . no one else knew what Thing had done.

Good.

But neither me nor Jackson knew what to do about it.

Bad . . .

'Mmmfffff!' Mrs Sweeney mumbled now, her face practically purple with shock and her eyes wide, white and bright as headlights.

And those eyes were fixed not so much on us standing there in our gym kits, but on the eerily moving bump under Jackson's T-shirt.

I could see what Mrs Sweeney was thinking. She'd already been held hostage by wild noodles – what on earth was going to burst out of Jackson's tum, and what exactly did it plan on doing to her?!?

And then meanie Sweeney's eyes nearly *popped* out of her head when Thing *popped* out from under Jackson's T-shirt.

'Thing, you've got to fix all this!' Jackson pleaded, grabbing hold of it and setting it down on the nearest table. 'Make those noodles disappear!'

'Eep!' Thing squeaked in reply, rubbing its tiny paws together nervously.

'Of *course* it can't fix what's happened!!' I said, as I went over to Mrs

Sweeney and started to unravel the ribbons of wobbly pasta from around her. 'Jackson, you *know* Thing needs to feel ARRGHH! before it can do any magic!'

'Well, yeah, but can't we do something to *make* it feel—'

Jackson didn't get to the end of his sentence. Like an eel wiggling through water, the section of noodles around Mrs Sweeney's mouth floated off into the air as I tugged at it.

'*What*,' she bellowed, 'is that flea-ridden, germ-infested *squirrel* doing in MY dining room!!'

Now, there was something very important that Mrs Sweeney didn't happen to know, and it's this: Thing *hates* squirrels.

And you must never, *ever* suggest that Thing is a squirrel, *even* if you think it looks a tiny bit like one. (Shh!)

And of course Mrs Sweeney also didn't know that Thing could talk.

'You – you *not* nice lady!' said Thing, suddenly trembling with *ARRGHH!* '*Not* nice words in your mouth!'

At the sound of Thing's funny purry voice, Mrs Sweeney gasped a huge gasp – and immediately fainted where she sat.

Which meant, of course, that she missed the seriously spectacular weirdness that was starting . . .

'What are you doing, Thing?' Jackson asked nervously.

'I make tornado . . . spin this not nice lady *away*!' Thing growled.

Flickers of light danced around the dining hall.

'*Please* don't!' I said uselessly, panicking about how we were going to hide a sudden, ferocious indoor storm from the rest of the school.

But it was too late for pleases, since sparkles were cartwheeling all around us.

And then just as soon as the mini fireworks show started, it stopped.

Then something else *began*; the overhead sprinkler system burst into life, sending lookalike showers of rain over us, over the whole dining room, over meanie Mrs Sweeney, our school's very own gloomy storm-cloud.

Wait a minute – I could *see* the droplets all around, but I couldn't *feel* them.

I was *dry*, and so was Jackson. So was a startled-looking Thing. It was as if we all had invisible umbrellas hovering above us.

Hold on; there was something a bit odd about the sprinkler rain. It was *steaming*. Which meant . . .

'The water's hot!' I blurted out in surprise.

Well, this wasn't exactly a tornado (thankfully), but then again, how could hot rain help us out of our sticky situation?

'Rubby! Boy! Look – noodle-doodles *deaded*!' Thing squeaked.

It was right.

The giant pasta ropes were shrinking to string-sized bits of spaghetti and flopping limp and lifeless onto the floor.

They'd been overcooked in the sprinkler water, turning from monster pasta to gluey mush, just like they'd been on my plate at lunchtime!

But what about Mrs Sweeney?

Phew – she seemed dry, same as us.

(Trying to explain a boiled catering assistant sounded *way* too complicated.)

'Help!'

'What?'

'*Eeeek!!*'

Uh-oh. From the shocked and startled cries coming from the direction of the kitchen, I realised that the sprinkler system had gone off in there too. Which meant it would only be a matter of *seconds* before the catering staff came hurtling out here to see what was going on.

'You, me and Thing,' I said to Jackson,

'*have* to get to the sick-room, *quick!*'

'But what if Mrs Sweeney tells on us?' Jackson worried, shovelling Thing into the rucksack so quickly that it squeaked in surprise.

The temperature was cooling; the water was turning from hot to cold; the sprinklers were turning themselves off . . .

'Let's see,' I said, pretending to mull over his dumb question as we splashed through lino puddles and headed out into the playground. 'Mrs Sweeney wakes up and tells everyone that the noodles came alive and tied her to a chair, and then *we* walked in with a talking squirrel!'

'I get it! They're going to think she's gone

absolutely and *totally* bananas, aren't they?'
Jackson grinned, knowing we were safe, safe
safe.

Though there was just *one* little problem.

Mrs Sweeney *might* not tell the whole
truth to the rest of the staff, in case they
thought she was bonkers. (And the staff *might*
think she'd just fainted, dropping all the
noodles on the floor, and that the sprinklers
came on by some faulty coincidence.)

But what was going to happen next time
me and Jackson were in the queue for lunch?

Was Mrs Sweeney going to silently punish
us for messing with her mind?

Would she make Jackson write out the
dining hall rules a hundred times?

And was *I* going to get served lettuce with
everything for the rest of my school life?

Apple pie, custard and lettuce; I couldn't
wait . . .

10
Very good sad news

At the end of Friday morning's assembly the Head Teacher made an announcement.

He had some sad news, he said.

Which turned out to be very *good* news for me and Jackson. *And* anyone else who had ever been growled at by Mrs Sweeney during lunch hours. (Which meant *everyone*, of course.)

Mrs Sweeney, the Head told us, had decided to take some time off, and think about a new career. 'Hey, maybe she could model for Halloween masks?!' Jackson whispered to me. I had to turn my snorty laugh into a choky sort of cough quick, before Miss Wilson told me off . . .

The new dinner lady was as different from Mrs Sweeney as butterflies are from pterodactyls.

'Hello, there! Just call me Shirley! Now what would you like today, dear? No problem!' she beamed at us all, while every single kid in school stared back open-mouthed, completely stunned by her niceness.

Of course we told Thing the very good sad news when we snuck down to the trees after school today.

'I *swish* I see Just-call-me-Shirley,' it had purred.

Quick as a blink, Jackson rifled in the

rustly bag in his hand, and offered Thing a yellow jellybaby.

In case you hadn't guessed, *yes*, Jackson was trying to distract it. That's because neither of us wanted Thing to think about . . . going anywhere *near* school ever again, or . . . going anywhere *else* in the big, wide world ever again.

So, to make its hideaway home in the straggle of trees seem extra homely and too-good-to-leave, me and Jackson had come armed with a couple of very special gifts.

As you'll see . . .

'Wheeeee!'

Thanks to the first gift, Thing had learned a new word.

It was wheeeeeing because it liked its trampoline very much.

I just hoped Jackson's mum didn't notice that her cake tin was missing any time soon.

And I'd have to tell Dad that I'd lost my
swimming cap next time he took me to the
pool.

'Boing!!' Thing squeaked, as it bounced
on the stretched red rubber, watched by
Christine cat, who was sitting on the stone
wall of my garden. Actually, no, she was just
sleeping, as usual.

'Hey, Thing – where do you want this?'

asked Jackson, holding up a picture of a tamarin monkey.

Jackson had downloaded it and then used his dad's laminator so that the print would stay nice and dry outdoors.

'That tree *good* tree!' purred Thing, pointing to a spindly sapling. 'Can see tammy monkey from my *house*, see?'

Ah, yes. If Jackson pinned the photo up right there, Thing could lie in its snug, rustly, crunchy bed inside the Scooby-Doo

Mystery Machine van and happily daydream about Amazonian rainforests.

'And I can go to the library in town tomorrow and get you a book about tropical habitats, if you like!' I suggested brightly.

I didn't expect Thing to react how it did.

'But Rubby, I not *like* snacks!' it said, wobbling to a quivering stop.

What, did yellow jelly babies and trampolines = travel sickness, perhaps?

'Don't worry, Thing!' said Jackson, while trying not to smirk. 'I'm sure Ruby will flip past any poisonous snacks in the book!'

Thing meant *snakes*! Well, hurray for Jackson being able to translate Thing-isms . . .

'Oh no, we definitely won't look at any of *those*!!' I chipped in, giving our ginger furry friend a comforting stroke on the back (and on those odd, useless stubby wings).

'Here, have *another* jellybaby,' said Jackson,

trying to cheer Thing up in his own, sweet-toothed way.

'Yes, please,' said Thing, helping itself to a handful. 'Rubby and boy *nice* to me – give me little people to eat *and* tammy monkey picture *and* trampling. Now I like to do nice to *you*!'

Uh-oh.

I hoped Thing wasn't about to give us any 'pressles'.

Last time it did, Jackson got a lovely gift of a stick, while I ended up with a handful of grass and some muddy knickers. (Don't ask.)

Before Thing could think of something we really didn't want or need, I came up with an idea.

'Hey, you know what would be really nice?' I said.

'Yes, please, Rubby?' said Thing, excitedly rocking from side to side.

'I'd love to see you fly!'

Stroking its back had given me the idea, of course.

'But Rubby, you know wingles not *ever* work!' Thing blinked up at me.

'Wow, I'd love to see you fly too!' Jackson joined in. 'Jump as high as you can, then wiggle those wingles!'

Thing blinked, dropped its semi-nibbled haul of sweets, and began bouncing.

Boing!

'Go on!' I said in my best encouraging voice. 'You can do it!'

Boing!

'Wiggle, wiggle, wiggle!' chanted Jackson.

Boing!

'Peh!' grunted Thing, with the effort of bouncing, not to mention the knobbly wing wobbling.

Boing!

'There! I'm sure I saw the left one move!'
Jackson burst out.

Boing!

'Rubby! I **FLY**! See?!' Thing purred
happily.

Me and Jackson clapped our hands
together so loudly that we nearly woke up

BOING!

Christine cat (but not quite).

In that same second, Jackson looked at me and I looked at Jackson.

And we both knew in that one little look that . . .

a) neither of Thing's stubby wings had moved a muscle, and . . .

b) nothing would make us happier than making our Thing happy. Even if that took a little white lie . . . .

And so that's the end of my story.

A story of the time when me and Jackson and Thing got away with not-so-secret snoring, toilets full of tomatoes, assorted paint gloopings and some very badly behaved noodle-doodles.

Luckily, Thing never got us into that sort of trouble again.

I swish!!

you, me and Thing

The Curse of the Jelly Babies

Hello.

I'm Ruby.

Can you keep a secret?

At the bottom of my garden lives a strange, small something.

Only me and Jackson Miller know about it. But Thing is a hard secret to keep, what with all the curses and jelly babies and stuff.

You won't tell, will you?

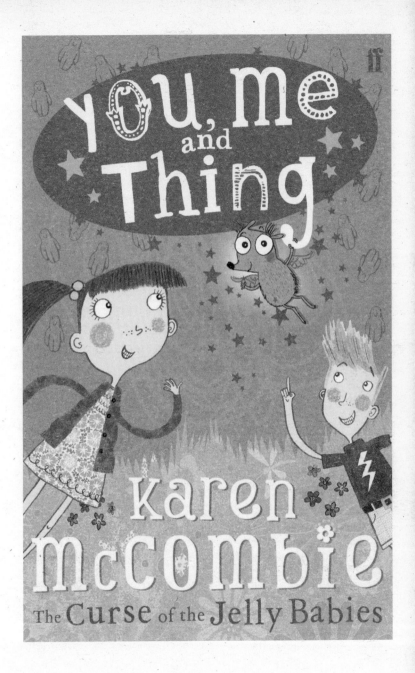